Alive and SCREAMING

A Collection
of Short Stories

Helen McCourt Mentek

Other books by Helen McCourt Mentek:

Ripples On A Puddle (2004)
See How They Die (2009)

Table of Contents

FriesenPress

Suite 300 - 990 Fort St
Victoria, BC, V8V 3K2
Canada

www.friesenpress.com

Copyright © 2018 by Helen McCourt Mentek
First Edition — 2018

ISBN
978-1-5255-1464-7 (Hardcover)
978-1-5255-1465-4 (Paperback)
978-1-5255-1466-1 (eBook)

1. FICTION, MEN'S ADVENTURE

Distributed to the trade by The Ingram Book Company

Acknowledgments

Thank you to my family and many friends for
their encouragement and support

John Mentek
Kathleen Allisen
Chris Mentek
Jenna Mentek
Michele Shields

The Shoah

One million pairs of tender feet
Marching in childish innocence
To their final destination

Guttural shouts sorting families like cattle
"You to the right. You to the showers."
Snaking down the path to a gaping iron door

Into the furnace of sacrifice
The door clangs shut
With the awful finality of death

Clothes shed, neatly sorted
Order within disorder
A paradox of madness.

Without warning
Death rains down
In a shower of poison

Helen McCourt Mentek

Owl-eyed naked children
Trembling in terror
Shrink against their mothers

Struggle to breathe the putrid air
Drowning in a virulent haze
WHERE WAS GOD?

II

This day,
Towering palms
Straight and steadfast as sentinels

Guard a crypt-like shrine
Clawed from the earth
An eternal witness to a lost generation
Sucked up like drops of rain on the desert sands

Enter, if you dare
A million beads of light
Glow from above in the darkness
Silver peepholes on the floor of heaven
One little star for one lost soul
Guided by angels to Paradise

Alive and Screaming

In the thick, black silence
A voice burdened with grief
Cries out to the world
Names, ages, homelands
Reciting their brief earthly presence
A grisly roll call for posterity

WHERE WERE WE?

Aaron's Journey

The clatter of heavy boots thundering up the stairs warned Anna Beck there was trouble coming. She met her husband Jacob's eyes. "They have come," she said. Her unsteady voice was a mixture of foreboding and fear. Jacob pointed to their eleven-year old son, Aaron, sitting on the window seat, and to the small cupboard beneath. Anna seized the boy and pushed him inside. At eleven years, Aaron was small for his age, and could squeeze his thin body into the small space. His parents had practiced this, so Aaron knew the drill. Finger to her lips, Anna cautioned him to stay quiet. Seconds later, two Nazi soldiers kicked in the door, rifles leveled at the terrified couple.

"Raus," they screamed, waving the couple back with their guns.

They ransacked the small apartment in less than five minutes, emptying the closets, banging on the walls, pulling up loose floor boards. Jacob moved to the front of the cupboard in a vain attempt to hide his son inside. But he only succeeded in drawing the attention of one of the soldiers, who shoved him roughly aside, jerking open the door. Aaron looked up, his eyes wide with fright. The soldier prodded the terrified boy out with his gun, "Come out of there Snowflake," he snarled in German, a reference to the ashes that fell from the chimneys when the dead were burned in the crematorium.

The soldiers pushed the family down the stairs and out into the street. A truck was waiting at the curb, crowded with men, women and children from their Berlin neighbourhood.

"Where are we going, mama?" Aaron asked, frightened by the brutality of the soldiers.

Anna gathered her son in her arms and held him close, as if she could protect him from the horrors she believed were soon to come.

"Hush child. We'll talk later." Rumours of Nazi death camps had been circulating for years throughout the Berlin ghetto. Many people had simply disappeared from their homes overnight. It was assumed they had been sent to the dreaded camps. What had happened to them there was unimaginable to those left behind.

Jacob held protective arms around his wife and son, as they sat, packed together with a dozen or so other families uprooted from their homes. The truck rumbled off, picking up speed. There was a train to catch.

At the railway station they joined hundreds of detainees gathered on the platform, their meagre belongings strewn before them. The silence of dread was heavy among them, as Nazi guards announced over loudspeakers that everyone would be "resettled" in the Ukraine. Their staccato commands and the snapping, growling dogs suggested a different story. Whatever the purpose of the announcement, Jacob took no solace in it, and believed nothing. He carried Aaron in his arms as he and Anna were ordered into a cattle car already overflowing with people. The door slammed shut, and the train lurched ahead. There was no room to sit. The crush of bodies kept most people standing. For three days they traveled without food or water. The sounds of wailing and sobbing, babies and children crying from hunger and thirst, mingled with the insufferable heat. Each day empty spaces to sit appeared on the floor, freed up by the old and the sick who had died during the night.

The dead bodies were stacked at the back of the car, where they lay in various stages of decay. Soon the car was filled with an unbearable stench, mingling with the stink of human waste. Mothers tried to quiet screaming children. Men with grim faces debated their fate.

Surely hell could not be worse than this.

Anna held a terrified Aaron tightly in her arms in a vain attempt to soothe him from the chaos around them. On the afternoon of the third day, the train finally screeched to a halt. The door flew open and everyone was ordered out. Those who could still move scrambled to the ground. Those who had died during the night were still standing, wedged in the midst of the living. The sick and the dead were left inside to be buried or burned later. The strong helped the weak escape the suffocating heat, and the sickening smell that permeated the car. The fresh air was so welcome they almost lost sight of the events that lay before them. As they left the train, the crowd stared in disbelief at the large hand-painted sign hanging over the camp's gate. The realization they had arrived at Treblinka death camp in Poland, instead of the Ukraine, was shattering.

It was September, 1941.

Anna, Jacob and Aaron clung together as they were forced down a narrow path and into a small clearing. Nazi soldiers divided them into two groups. Those who could work were separated from those who were too weak or too young to be useful. Jacob was selected with a group of men and older boys for the camp workforce, while Anna and Aaron were propelled down the path with the women, children and the infirm. Jacob was assigned to sort the clothing left in the storage shed by the prisoners, who trustingly had walked naked into the gas chamber, believing that they would simply be having a shower.

Outside, the air was thick with fumes and smoke blocked out the sun, turning the bright September day into gloomy twilight. The crowd of people moving down the path stopped before a large brick building. Anna gasped in horror. She could see the building was too small to house everyone. Was this the rumoured crematorium? Unable to say goodbye to Jacob, her only thought now was to save Aaron, holding tightly to her hand.

She looked around frantically but could see no place to hide him. The line kept moving relentlessly, and people began disappearing into the building. Anna was desperate. Carried along with the crowd, she noticed a wooden rain barrel standing near the entrance. Little did she know that the Nazis collected rainwater to wash away the blood and excrement from inside the building, after the prisoners were suffocated by the carbon monoxide fumes piped into the 'showers'. The dead bodies were then taken away by forced labourers and buried in a pit of lime.

Instinctively, Anna seized on the rain barrel as the only hope to hide Aaron. It was so slim a chance, she could not bring herself to question it. She saw this as the only possible way to save her son. The lone guard had returned to the end of the long line.

"Aaron," she leaned down to the boy, her voice barely audible. "Do you see that rain barrel over by the building?" Aaron nodded. Keeping her voice low, she continued. "When the guard is out of our sight, run to it as fast as you can and climb in. Keep your head above the water. When he starts to come back I will signal for you to duck under. Stay down until he leaves again. Don't let him see you. I'll be watchful of his movements."

"Where will you be, mama?" he asked, his voice trembling with fear.

"Don't worry little one," his mother whispered. "Just listen to me. When night comes, everyone will be gone. Climb out! Run for the fence. Climb up. Run hard for the woods. Hide yourself...find someone to help you. I will come to you later."

In truth Anna knew she would never come to him. She gazed at him with tears in her eyes, holding back her grief.

The guard walked along the line shouting "No talking. Keep moving." He turned around and walked back out of sight.

"Go now." Anna pushed Aaron out of the line. With speed fueled by terror, Aaron ran to the rain barrel. Others in line watched in dismay as he boosted his small body into it. An old man standing in the queue whispered, "God go with you, son."

The water was cold. Aaron sank down under the scum and waited until he could hold his breath no longer. He raised himself and peered over the rim at his mother. Anna heard the guard shouting as he walked back to the head of the line. She quickly pointed downward, and Aaron disappeared under the water. When he looked again the line had dwindled to a dozen or so people, and he did not see his mother. The last of the line was moving into the building. He stood trembling in the water, despair overtaking him. He was very frightened, but he resolved to carry out the plan has mother had set in motion for him. He listened for the guard but heard nothing.

When darkness fell hours later, he slowly raised himself on tiptoe above the water and looked around, his ears alert to the slightest noise. Reassured, he climbed out, cold and shivering. He hid behind the barrel for a few minutes half-expecting to be discovered, but there was no one in sight. It seemed everyone was asleep. Even the guard dogs were silent, chained and kenneled for the night. He emptied his water-filled boots, tied the laces together and hung them around his neck. Then he sprinted off, running to a part of the fence hidden behind the crematorium.

The fence was ten feet high, an almost insurmountable goal to a four-foot boy. But he had to get over it. And climb it he did, with all the strength in his frail body.

Dirty and wet, he dropped down to the other side, barefoot and gasping for breath. He ran and fell, ran and fell, until he was deep into the woods. Trembling with fear and exhaustion, he couldn't run any farther and threw himself onto a bed of dry leaves on the forest floor.

Scarcely able to raise his arms, he scooped the leaves over his body, burying himself on the moist earth. His wet clothes clung to him like a thousand leeches as he trembled in the cold night air. Soon he drifted into a state of semi-consciousness.

In the morning, with sunlight splintering through the foliage, he awoke to the chattering of a few noisy crows. Cautiously he pushed the blanket of leaves aside and looked around.

The forest was dreary and damp, the dead autumn leaves drooping wetly from the trees. He crawled over to a patch of sun and lay down, relishing the warmth. His boots were still wet, but it was better than walking barefoot over stones and tree branches. He was very hungry and his thirst was unrelenting. He tried to quench it by licking the morning dew from the leaves of the trees as he walked along.

A patch of dandelions caught his eye. He made a face, remembering how his mother had often put them in a bowl of greens with their nightly meal. He always hated them, and would secretly slide them off his plate when she wasn't looking. But now he was so hungry he picked and ate a few, grimacing at their sharp taste. His damp clothes still clung to his skin so he lay down in a patch of sun and tried to decide what to do next. He knew he had to get as far away as he could from that camp and its deadly business. He was very lonely for his mother and father. He felt his father would be safe as a worker in the camp, but his mother... he put those uneasy thoughts out of his mind for now.

He walked on hoping to find someone he could trust, just as his mother had instructed, and prayed she would find him soon. Trudging on, unsure of his destination, he picked dandelions and acorns to eat. He stuffed mushrooms in his pockets, remembering how his father had taught him to tell the good ones from the bad. It seemed a very long time since he had picked mushrooms with his father. He dropped some pieces along his path as he walked, hoping his mother would understand his feeble attempt to signal her when she came for him.

At dusk, he started looking for a safe place to sleep. Some fallen tree branches gave him an idea for a hiding place. He scraped out a hollow in the ground with a stick, filled it with dry leaves and pulled some of the smaller branches over it. Then he slid underneath and covered himself with the leaves. He was well hidden for the night. He ate some of the mushrooms and dandelions, but exhaustion soon claimed him and he fell into a deep sleep.

He awakened to a warm sun breaking through chinks in the forest canopy. He opened his eyes and began to push aside the branches, when he heard a dog barking. A man's voice was shouting. Aaron grew numb with fright.

"Max, Max, Szybciej Spiesze sie (Come! I'm in a hurry)!" The man was speaking Polish, and the words made no sense to Aaron, but their harsh sounds rang out like those of the bellowing Nazi soldiers.

The dog sensed something under the branches. He came closer, sniffing the area and then barking and jumping excitedly. The man shouted again, but the dog ignored him and continued to dance around the site. Aaron was afraid the racket would bring the man closer, and when he heard the rustling of approaching footsteps, he began to panic. His breath came in gasps, and he squeezed his eyes and mouth shut. He felt the branches being pulled away.

He lay still, eyes tightly closed, feigning death. The man bent down and touched him softly on the cheek, and in Aaron's very knowing experience, this gentleness was not the way of a soldier. He opened his eyes cautiously.

It was not a man in a Nazi uniform leaning over him, but an old man in a black cassock that swayed gently in the light breeze. A square cap on his head was slightly askew, white hair sprouting out from under it like bits of straw. Aaron stared owl-eyed into the pale face of a tall and very thin priest, who peered down at him, calling out in Polish.

"Are you alive, child?" He touched the boy's forehead, and it felt warm with life. Aaron's heart was pounding. He opened his mouth but no sound came.

"I'm Father Anders, son. Who are you and why are you hiding?" Aaron was too terrified to speak.

"Don't be frightened, child. I will not hurt you. Let me help you out of there." Still speaking Polish and with no response, he assumed the boy didn't understand him. He gestured with his hand for the boy to sit up. Aaron struggled to his knees and Father Anders lifted his slender figure out of the leaves.

Max was sniffing around the boy, wagging his tail in a friendly manner. Aaron walked slowly with the priest through the forest as he described his escape from the camp. The priest bent his head in concentration. Although the boy was speaking in German, punctuated with Yiddish inflections, Father Anders easily pieced together Aaron's story. As a young curate in Cologne, the priest had learned to speak a German dialect. He uttered words of solace as the boy timidly related what had happened to his parents. By now Aaron felt reassured that the priest was someone he could trust.

As they walked through the woods together, Max bounded along beside them, oblivious to the gravity of their conversation.

Leaving the woods, Aaron was suddenly overcome by hunger and exhaustion and fell to the ground in a dead faint. The priest gathered his limp body in his arms and carried him to the church rectory in the village of Treblinka.

The streets were empty. Everyone was fearful of leaving their homes. German patrols were everywhere in the town and they could arrest anyone for no reason.

A startled Mrs. Sobieski, the housekeeper, opened the rectory door to them.

"Who is this boy, Father?" she asked, clasping her hands together. When she spoke Polish, Aaron's eyes flew open in fright. He began to whimper.

"You're safe now son," Father Anders assured him. He carried the frail boy into the kitchen and sat down, cradling him in his arms. His housekeeper stared down at the priest, her eyes calling for an explanation.

"Max discovered him hiding in the woods, Pani. He escaped alone from the prison camp. He is in great danger of being sent back to his death if he is caught." The housekeeper looked at him curiously.

"He is Jewish, you see," the Father explained. "He was taken there with his parents, but by some miracle he managed to escape. He will tell you all about it, in his way, but now I want to get him some food. The boy is starving. He's been living on acorns and mushrooms in the forest. And something for him to drink right away, please Pani. He is totally dehydrated." The housekeeper bustled about the kitchen preparing a plate of food. The priest placed the boy on a bed in a spare room where he instantly fell asleep. Hours later he awoke to a meal such as he had never had, and a bath he desperately needed. The housekeeper gave him a blanket to cover himself and set about washing his filthy clothes.

Aaron stayed hidden in the rectory for three weeks until Father Anders could make contact with the Polish Resistance. The old priest had many friends in the Resistance from his involvement in assisting other escapees. Aaron was given false documents and a new Polish name. A record of his legal name, Aaron Beck, and his new Polish name, Karol Nowak, along with details of his escape, were carefully hidden in the rectory in the hope that someday he could be reunited with surviving members of his family.

He was escorted overland by various underground cells and smuggled out of the country into England, where he was placed in a home for refugee children. He lived in the home for four years. When the war ended in 1945, he was adopted by a family in Coventry, where he attended school for the first time. He was fifteen years old. Over the years, he made many attempts to find his parents and Father Anders. He checked hundreds of lists of survivors. He found no mention of his mother or father but learned that Father Anders had died during the war.

He was a bright, diligent student and quickly made up for lost time, graduating at the top of his classes. Defying many obstacles Aaron became a well-educated man, and determined to move forward in his life as Karol Nowak.

He left university with a doctorate in modern history, and was hired to lecture at Cambridge University, where he remained for more than twenty years.

Here he became acquainted with many refugees, and always sought out information about his parents, never forgetting who he really was.

In the fall of 1974, he was scanning a list of students registered for his history class.

One name piqued his curiosity. He wondered if the 'Jacob Beck' on his list could possibly have some connection to his lost family. He asked his secretary to invite the student to his office.

Jacob Beck arrived at his door somewhat unnerved. He hoped there was nothing wrong with his credentials for the course. He knocked softly.

"Come in," Karol beckoned as Jacob appeared tentatively in the doorway. "Please come in and sit down Jacob, and don't be nervous. I am only curious about your background. I realize there are many families with the name Beck in Berlin, but I would like to know if you have a connection to a family I knew there before the war and have been unable to locate. Would you mind telling me a little about yourself?"

"Not at all," he said, relieved at the turn the conversation had taken.

"My father, Jacob Beck, was arrested in Berlin along with his wife and son. They were sent to the Treblinka death camp. When the war ended in 1945, he was released by the Allies and he returned to Berlin. He searched for information about his son for years but never found any trace of him. He knew his wife had been gassed the day the family arrived at the camp. He was ordered to sort through the belongings of prisoners who had been killed, to save any valuables. He found the black and white checked coat she was wearing. He told me he held the coat to his face, breathing in the last traces of her life, and knew she was gone. I think he wanted to die right there with her."

Karol stifled a cry as he recalled his mother's promise to come to him after his escape. For a long time, he suspected she may have died, but he always held out a glimmer of hope he might find her alive. Now he knew the truth. His shoulders shook and his eyes filled.

Jacob was not surprised by this reaction to his family tragedy. So many families lived with their own painful stories, emotions barely in check. He waited patiently for Professor Nowak to regain his composure, and then continued.

"Later, in Berlin, my father met my mother, Ruth Varka. She'd been a prisoner at Sobibor. They married shortly after, and moved to London where I was born. They're still there. Unfortunately, Dad was never able to find out what happened to his son."

Karol could wait no longer. "Can you tell me his son's name?"

"His son's name was Aaron. He was only 11 years old when they were taken. Knowing how Anna—that's his first wife—had died, Dad finally accepted that Aaron must have died with her."

When Karol was able to catch his breath, he said, "Well, Jacob, I am that Aaron Beck... and I'm very much alive."

Jacob stared at the professor in surprise.

"I ran away from Treblinka in 1941 and hid in a forest. I was given a new name by a Polish priest who found me hiding and arranged my escape to England. That's why my father could never find me. He was looking for Aaron Beck."

The room fell silent as the news sank in. Then Karol spoke again.

"Do you know what this means Jacob?"

"I...I think so sir. I believe it means we are half-brothers," the young man stammered.

Both men suddenly smiled.

"Indeed it does," said Karol. He jumped up from his chair to take his brother's outstretched hand.

Being reunited with his father would bring the gift of a new-found family. It was incredible to think they had lived so close to one another all these years, and that the long-lost son would soon be returned to his family as Professor Karol Nowak.

Napalm Girl

"Take courage, daughter. Your faith has healed you."
Matthew 9:22

Hot breezes ruffle the tender green shoots
A mid-day sun splinters eager eyes
Shaded with wide-brimmed raffia hats
A family labours silently
Tending their fragile plants
From out of the heavens a dreaded drone
Rumbles closer
Four aircraft surge from the clouds
Like fourwinged pterodactyls
Roaring, spitting, convulsing the earth
Four monstrous eggs
Float gently down
Striking the scorched red earth
Bursting into flashes of orange jelly
Sticking like yolk to tender skins
Soft flesh burning, tiny bones melting
Childish screams rend the air
"Too hot, too hot" they cry

Helen McCourt Mentek

Clothes sucked off, cremated
Running, running naked
Soldiers watch in helpless horror
As the panorama unfolds

Time rolled on
A young woman
Scarred in body
But flawless of soul
Speaks a message of faith
"I forgive you"

Heavy Baggage

The guns fell silent. The whirring sounds of helicopters carrying the dead and wounded faded into the distance. The war-weary survivors of the reconnaissance platoon made a hasty retreat into the jungle mists, after a major defeat in a firefight with the enemy. Last to leave the clearing was Sgt. Mario Petroni. As he ran for cover, a bullet caught him before he could reach the woods. He lay a few meters beyond the tree line in the open field, his leg wounded and bleeding. One of the remaining survivors in the platoon called for a rescue helicopter. When the enemy appeared to have abandoned the scene, a young medic darted out of the woods, and pulled the Sgt. to safety. Mario's M14 lay glinting in the open field. Ever mindful of the army's constant warnings, "Don't leave anything for the enemy," the medic ran back to the clearing to retrieve the weapon.

Mario saw him go and shouted, "Leave it! Come back!" But it was too late. A lone sniper's bullet caught him as he zig-zagged across the field. The bullet went straight to his heart, killing him instantly. For a split second, Mario wished it was him. He never even knew the fellow's name. He was just "the new guy", who'd arrived that morning to replace one who had been gunned down yesterday. Lately, the replacements coming in were very young and ill-trained, and almost always died or were injured within a month of their arrival.

This morning, the fighting had been so intense there was no time to learn anything about him. And now it was too late, and everyone was too tired to care. Someone shouted, "Bird comin'," as a rescue helicopter flapped overhead and dropped down at the edge of the clearing. Gunners were poised inside the open doors to cover the two rescue volunteers emerging from the woods. They loaded the medic's body into one of the rescue baskets. Mario was placed inside the helicopter, where a medic gave his leg wound immediate attention. As the pilot lifted off for the nearby mobile hospital, Mario lay inside worrying about Lillian, his wife, back home in the States hearing the news of his injury. He felt horrible, imagining her agonizing about him. The army was never big on details and she would probably think the worst. In the short months they'd been together, he knew his wife to be strong and sensible. He prayed that she would not be too distressed.

Lillian Johnson had known Mario Petroni since high school. She'd always been struck by his handsome Italian appearance and happy-go-lucky manner, but she'd never got to know him personally. Not that she hadn't tried. He was friendly enough whenever they'd met, but that was all. After high school, he'd left Yorkville, the town where they had both grown up. He went to Williamsville, a town about four hundred miles east to look for work.

For several years he lived there, working in one of the town's factories. In Yorkville, Lillian had heard very little about him, but she never forgot him. Then one day he turned up back in Yorkville, dressed in the uniform of an American marine. He was a tall handsome man, in his mid-twenties.

By chance, he walked into the restaurant where Lillian was having lunch with some friends. Her surprise and delight at seeing him was evident to all at the table. They remembered the heavy crush she'd had on him in high school. They teased her mercilessly. "Your knight in shining armour has returned, Lil," they laughed. "He's come back to carry you off and ravish you." Lillian ignored their teasing and called out to him.

"Hey, Mario. Come and join us."

Mario turned around to see Lillian eagerly beckoning him. A huge grin covered his face.

"Well," he said, coming toward her, "how are ya, Lil? You're lookin' great!"

"What are you doing back in town, Mario Petroni?" she asked, playfully.

"Well," he said, "I had some leave so I came back to see my family, and some of my old buddies. But now that I've seen you, I think I'll give them all a pass," he teased.

He drew up a chair and sat down beside her. She immediately began peppering him with questions. "Why are you wearing an American uniform? Don't tell me you joined up, Mario. Are you crazy?!"

"I did, and I'm not. I love it in the Marines. You know me. Always looking for something new and exciting!"

She continued to badger him about his life, while her friends looked on with amusement. He declined her invitation to lunch, but wasted no time making a date with her for that night.

They met in the same restaurant for dinner. The hours flew by while they traded stories of their lives since leaving high school. By the end of the evening, Mario was totally smitten.

"Don't think you're going to get away from me," he laughed, as they left the restaurant. "I'll write to you, and I'll be back in Yorkville on my next leave." True to his promise, in the months that followed he made many trips to Yorkville from his army base in Ohio. They fell in love.

On his last visit, before he shipped out to Vietnam, he'd arranged to take her to an elegant restaurant out of town. Lillian had protested that it was far too expensive.

"Not this time, honey. Tonight is heavy." And he gave her a sly wink.

"What are you up to, Mario Petroni?" she demanded.

"Patience, my love. You'll see." But his gentle brush off didn't cover his anxiety about what he had planned. When Lillian excused herself to the ladies' room, Mario signaled the waiter, who brought over a bottle of champagne he had previously ordered. After filling their glasses, the waiter watched in amusement as Mario took a ring out of his pocket and dropped it into Lillian's glass.

"Good luck with that," the waiter said, smiling. When Lillian returned, Mario raised his glass in a toast.

"To us, Lil," Mario pledged. "You know how much I love you and now I'm asking you to marry me, if you'll have me." They each took a mouthful of the wine. Mario looked eagerly into her eyes awaiting her answer.

Lillian smiled at him. She took her time, sipping the wine while Mario sat in mounting suspense.

The seconds ticked by and still Lillian said nothing.

Mario was becoming worried.

Suppose she refused him. Or worse still, laughed at him. Then when she couldn't keep him in suspense any longer, she pulled his hands toward her, squeezing them hard, laughing at his worried look.

"Oh, Mario. Yes! Of course I'll marry you. I think I've loved you for a very long time. Even though you always ignored me!"

Mario was ecstatic. He lifted her hands to his lips. "I never did that! I always admired you. But today you've made me a very happy man, Lil."

Suddenly, he frowned at her. "Why'd you take so long to tell me?"

"Well," she answered, "I was thinking of you away in the army, and we'd be separated for who knows how long. I wondered if it was right for us to marry right now, with the war and everything. But then when I saw you so desperate for an answer, I just couldn't say anything but yes. She drained her glass and discovered the ring nestled on the bottom. She held it up, her eyes shining. "Oh, Mario, it's beautiful!"

she cried. He slipped it on her finger, leaned across the table, and kissed her tenderly.

Their wedding was small and quiet. It was what they both wanted, just family members and a few close friends. They rented a small house in Yorkville, and moved in with the help of their many friends. With Mario on leave, in their new home together, they fulfilled every day blissfully. But they were always aware of their impending separation. Then the dreaded news came. Within two months of their marriage, Mario's unit was deployed to Vietnam. A tearful Lillian said good-bye and began the long and lonely wait for the day he would return. She prayed every day that he would come back to her safely.

After the fall of Saigon the American troops were demobilized. Mario arrived back in Yorkville to his beloved Lillian.

At first, he felt like a stranger in his home. He discovered that saying good-bye was a lot easier than saying hello. The early days were difficult, as he tried to reconnect with his wife and their friends and get accustomed to a quiet life. Lillian tried her best to ease him back into the life he'd known before, and to not make too many demands on him, but he couldn't seem to let go of the war. When they went to restaurants, he would sit with his back to the wall. Rogue flashes of a man pointing a gun at him would pop into his head and he would become so agitated they would have to leave.

He was desperate to settle into a normal existence. For the first few months he seemed to be adjusting well on the surface, but it wasn't long before the horrific nightmares began to invade his sleep. They were like a tape playing in his head, over and over, acting out explosions and death until sleep abandoned him altogether. He spent the days coping with both being alive, and the guilt of having survived when so many of his buddies did not. Although his leg wound healed, the ache in his brain would not go away. A noise or smell could trigger a panic attack at any time or any place. He was constantly on edge, and Lillian could see that all was not right with him.

One afternoon she returned from shopping to find him sitting on the bed cutting his arms with a razor blade. Horrified and frightened, she pressed him for an answer.

"Mario, what are you doing?"

He looked up at her, his eyes full of anguish.

"Lil, you would never understand. If I tell you that it feels like all the pain is flowing out with my blood, would that make any sense to you? I don't think so."

He shook his head in despair.

"This is serious Mario," she said softly. "You have to get help right away."

"Don't you tell me what to do! You know nothing!" he said, and immediately regretted it. "Sorry, sorry love," he muttered, putting his arms around her.

"It's alright, my love," Lillian answered quietly.

Lillian kept insisting that he go immediately to their family doctor. A few days later, when the nightmares became too much for him to bear, he agreed. The doctor placed Mario under the care of a military physician who was treating other veterans for similar symptoms of war-related stress.

Mario was still in good physical condition and able to work, and he got a job in Yorkville's steel mill. He settled for a 'semi-normal' life with Lillian, whom he adored. For a few months, the daily effort of going to work helped to spare him some of the horrors of war. But it wasn't long before he began to feel trapped in his job. He became claustrophobic in the confined space where he worked. His thoughts grew to be totally irrational, and he believed he could never escape from the workplace because there was no way to escape his thoughts.

His distress triggered such pain that he was forced to quit his job. By day, horrific memories preyed on his mind. By night, Lillian was awakened by Mario thrashing and screaming, acting out an explosion in his dreams. When the picture faded, he would curl himself in a ball and remain like that for several minutes, gasping for breath.

He'd been home for six months but couldn't get the sights and sounds of war out of his head, and the smell of death from his nostrils. His sleep would end abruptly by the sound of a single rifle shot, and the sight of the young medic's body lying in the field. He would spring up in the bed and shout, "No! Come back!" Lillian would hold his trembling body, trying to comfort him.

And now, recently, an unrelated event had invaded his nightmares.

One morning, Mario lingered longer than usual at the breakfast table. He was very disturbed after a dreadful night filled with terror. Visions of a dead girl, blood oozing from her mouth and nose, and lying in a fetal position in a field, had crept into his sleep. The incident did happen many years past in the woods in Williamsville, and he'd almost forgotten about it. It was not connected to the war and it didn't make any sense showing up in his dreams. Finally, after repeated occurrences, he knew if he was to have any peace of mind, he had to know what happened to that girl who had died in the woods, and where he had been on that fateful night.

That morning Lillian was fussing around the kitchen.

"Are you all right, honey?" she asked, looking at him. "You're very quiet this morning. Is there something bothering you?"

Mario avoided her eyes. "Yeah, there's something I need to tell you, Lil." He spoke softly, pausing to collect his thoughts. "Do you remember when we first dated, I told you about a girl who died in the woods one night in Williamsville? It was before I joined the Marines."

Lillian nodded. "Yes, I remember." She watched him intently.

"Well," he paused and took a deep breath, "I think I may have killed her." He looked at her in desperation.

Lillian stared at him, speechless.

His voice dropped to a whisper. "I don't know how it happened, or why it happened, but I was the last one out of the woods that night.

Lately, I've been dreaming about the whole incident. In the dream, the whole scene seems to switch around. Sometimes it's the medic lying dead in the field in Nam, and sometimes it's the woman lying in the woods."

"Well, those dreams have nothing to do with each other," Lillian reassured him. "You have to tell your doctor what's going on." She could see he was deeply troubled by all of this. "Honey, try to put the war behind you now, and get on with your life."

"Oh, the war never leaves you, Lil. I wake up sweating it, feeling it and smelling it. You think because you're home, you're alright. But you're not. It never goes away. Even when I'm awake, I sometimes have flashes of dead bodies stretched out in rows on the ground, and I can smell the stink of rotting bodies all around me.

"And now I'm haunted by this dead girl, and I can't account for it. I know it happened, Lil. It replays over and over, as if I was back there in Williamsville with that mob of drunken people. In the dream, there seem to be dead bodies everywhere, just like in Nam. The whole thing is crazy."

"Mario," Lillian said tenderly, "I've known you forever and I just can't see you doing anything to hurt this young girl ... and for what reason, if you didn't even know her? Look dear, we'll just have to find out more about what happened to the girl and who she was. We'll go to the newspaper office in Williamsville and see what we can dig up. If there's nothing there, we'll go to the police. They must have a record of it. You have to get to the bottom of this, Mario, before it drives you crazy."

A week later, they met with the librarian of the Williamsville newspaper. "About 20 years ago?" she said. "Let's see what we can turn up."

She opened the files to the approximate time and date Mario recalled. They looked through many pages of copy. Mario had almost given up.

"Is this what you're looking for?" She read out the headline: *"Local girl found dead in woods"*

"Oh, this has to be it," Mario said. Reading the account, his thoughts took him back to that night, when he dropped into a local tavern for a drink after work. Bits of memory began to creep back. He remembered the proprietor was preparing to close. A small band of local musicians were packing up their instruments. Boisterous patrons were well on their way to inebriation when they were driven out into the night. The normally deserted streets became busy, as knots of noisy imbibers merged into a stream of figures, churning toward Epps woods at the edge of town. Their raucous shouting and singing pierced the night air.

Mario was swept into the throng as it swung into the woods. The rowdy crowd suddenly erupted into a free-for-all, ignited by a rivalry for the attentions of a girl in the crowd. In the ensuing melee, Mario was struck in the face by a flying fist and fell to the ground, whacking his head on a log. When he regained consciousness some hours later, everyone had left. He struggled to his feet and stumbled out of the woods into the night. Staggering along the street in the dark, he reached his home and flung himself onto his bed. He slept for hours.

The following day, three boys playing in the woods discovered the body of a girl. Police questioned everyone who had been there that night, including Mario. The blood where he fell was examined and determined to be his. He was dismissed from the police interrogation along with all the others.

Police found no evidence of a homicide.

Later, an inquest ruled the mishap an accidental death, but by then, Mario had quit his job and joined the Marines.

The librarian was speaking again as she read from the newspaper:

"Amanda Fleck, daughter of George and Isabel Fleck, was found dead this morning in Epps Woods. An investigation concluded there was no evidence of foul play, and the Coroner confirmed that she had been caught

up in a brawl in the woods that night. It was presumed that she was accidentally knocked down and struck her head on a large rock. The blood on it was examined and found to be hers. The coroner determined that she died instantly of a brain injury."

The librarian stopped reading and looked at Mario and Lillian. Neither of them recognized the girl's photo in the paper.

Upon hearing all this, they felt their anxiety fade. Mario was freed from one of his torments, although the stress of the war remained for many years.

Over time, the night terrors eased their grip and Mario was able to return to work and support his family, which had grown to include three much-loved children. Lillian was always at his side, helping him through the tough times.

Mario came to realize he was a lucky man, not a victim. Love for his wife and family, and their unwavering love and support for him, slowly filled him with a deep contentment that shielded him from old wounds that never quite healed.

Alpine Glory

From a lofty windswept bridge
I sun-squint at distant
Lilliputian farmhouses
Thumbtacked randomly to mountain sides

Woolly clouds drift carelessly
Over snowy
Mountain tops
I contemplate the glorious spectacle
As it silently steals my logic

A mighty Gulliver
Invades my vision
He stands astride the glistening peaks
Straddling the valley below
Shouting hope to a troubled world

The Singing Cadavers

The snow had fallen steadily for hours. Gusts of it billowed, swirled and drifted, melting into beads of silver on his face. For several hours, medic Joe Nicholson lay undisturbed, his body buried beneath an icy blanket of white. As consciousness slowly intruded, he opened his eyes to a desolate world.

Blinking away the white specks on his eyelashes, he struggled to piece together the events that had brought him to this place. His eyes roamed over the eerie surroundings. He looked around for something familiar, his mind racing with questions. Where was he? The outline of the snow-covered Twin Otter quickly sharpened his memory of the sudden ominous silence that descended as the engines iced up and stalled, screams as the plane lurched and plunged from the sky, the pilot yelling, "sit tight, boys, it's gonna' be rough." Then nothing. On impact, Joe was flung out the plane's open door.

Carefully he turned his head. His eyes were drawn to three white mounds outlined in grotesque shapes a few feet from the plane. He was sure that underneath those heaps of snow were the bodies of the passengers and crew. He wondered if any were still alive.

He felt no pain as he gingerly moved his legs. It was a monumental effort to sit up, though, and he quickly fell back, struck by a blinding throbbing in his head. He cautiously touched his forehead. His glove came away smeared with blood from a deep gash. He fumbled under the snow, and found a half-buried tree branch. Gripping it firmly in both hands, he pushed himself to his feet.

Cupping his hands to his mouth he called out, "Hello, hello" ... but only his echo answered. The place was deadly silent. In fact, it seemed there was not another living thing as far as the eye could see—not even birds.

He crept over to the nearest snowdrift. The powdery stuff flew from his hand as he brushed it away, revealing the still face of Tim Mulcaster, the pilot. He knelt beside him and touched his neck, feeling for a pulse. There was none. His dread mounting, Joe moved over to the second mound. As he swept away the snow, the face of the Inuk woman was revealed, silent in death, still clutching her dead baby to her chest. The mother and baby had been evacuated from Baker Lake, NWT. The crew was flying them to Edmonton for medical treatment for the infant, who was suffering from a severe case of pneumonia. The woman's toothless mouth was set in a hideous scream, an effigy of terror that Joe couldn't bear to look at. He wanted to hide her fixed grimace and those wide-open unseeing eyes, frozen in fright. He covered her face with snow again, ashamed of his sudden revulsion.

"No need for a hospital now," he thought sadly. "Guess she finally gave up on the shaman. Not that it made any difference in the end." The Inuit consulted a shaman first before calling for the Medevacs. Often by that time, they were beyond medical help.

A few yards away, Joe let out a deep groan as he uncovered the face of his good friend, co-pilot Pete Bagley. Joe cried out in denial. "Oh, no, not you too, Pete!"

Pete's boyish face was as soft and vulnerable as a sleeping child. He was the youngest of the crew at twenty-three, and had just earned his wings, but his fate was sealed along with the others.

Joe sat back on his heels, his thoughts racing. "How did I survive?" he wondered, completely mystified. Then the 'what-if's' began to rattle around in his head.

"What if no one finds me before I freeze or starve to death?" A spasm of fear travelled through his body like an arrow, and his mouth dried up in panic. He was terribly aware that one of those two outcomes was a definite possibility.

Joe shook off his fear and with a grim face plodded unsteadily back to the Otter, his steps kicking up clouds of swirling white flakes. Groping around under Tim's seat, he pulled out the First Aid kit. He soaked a wad of cotton with antiseptic and touched the wound on his forehead, sucking in his breath as the liquid stung like fire. He pressed a Band-Aid over the cut.

He set about ransacking the plane's interior, tossing aside useless items as he searched for food and water. There was no telling when he would be rescued but rescue would come, he told himself. Any crumbs he could salvage might prolong his life while he waited. Under the co-pilot's seat he discovered a bottle of water and a bag of Cheezies. He pulled them out with a cry of triumph. "Thank-you Pete," he said, grateful that his friend's weakness for junk food had followed him into the cockpit.

Gulps of cold water eased his dry throat and a handful of Cheezies tamed his hunger for the moment. More searching yielded a tool kit and a working flashlight. He tried the radio but as he suspected, it was broken, ruling out any signal to his base in Yellowknife. He sat for a few moments trying to come up with a plan. It was mandatory procedure that a search and rescue operation would be sent out when contact was lost and the plane failed to arrive at the Edmonton hospital. Meanwhile, he needed to conserve his energy and the little food he had. His thirst could be quenched with snow and there was plenty of that.

He decided to make an SOS marker in the snow. He hauled pieces of the plane's shattered wreckage to a flat open area, and began to construct a crude signal. After an hour or so of heavy slogging, he stepped back to view his handiwork, nodding in satisfaction. A search party would surely recognize it for what it was, if he could only keep the snow from burying it.

Back inside the Otter, he felt the piercing wind sweep through the rubble of the plane. The shattered door rattled with each icy blast. Against the bone-chilling cold, Joe burrowed deeply into his down parka. He pulled a balaclava over his face and wrapped some emergency blankets around him. He felt reasonably comfortable, and settled down on the floor at the back of the plane, where there was some protection from the wind, and sank into a deep sleep.

He dreamed the cadavers buried in the snow nearby were calling out to him and singing his favourite songs, which the crew had been singing together on the flight before the crash. He awoke with their voices still ringing in his ears. He pressed his hands over his ears to try to block out the sound.

The day after the crash, he awoke to more drifting snow falling on his face. "Not another friggin' blizzard!" he groaned. He tossed aside his blankets, grabbed the flashlight and stumbled through the snow to his S.O.S. marker. His face was whipped by the wind, as he frantically scooped away snow from the primitive signal. But the effort was futile. It was coming down faster than he could brush it off. He decided to wait it out in the plane.

The brutal cold intensified until his hands and feet were nearly paralyzed. He unrolled a map and searched for his location but couldn't be sure. He was just the medic. The pilot had mapped out the course and he'd clearly gone off it.

Joe's stomach was growling. He ate a few more Cheezies and brooded, wondering how long before he'd be rescued, or if he'd be rescued at all before he surrendered to a frozen death. The fear made him nauseous. Although the air was freezing, his hands were sweating. He began to shake violently.

A steady drumming filled his ears. It seemed to transcend the ghostly silence surrounding him.

The bodies in the snow were calling again, urging him to join them.

He was becoming severely disoriented and reached out for something solid to grab onto. He sucked in deep breaths and counted each one as he fought the rising panic.

It was a relief when he finally passed out.

On day three, he awoke to find the snow had stopped. With faltering steps, he retraced his path to the SOS sign and slowly swept away the snow. His breath released white puffs in the frosty air. Feeling some consolation that his sign was again visible from the air, he dragged his weary body back to the plane. Pulling the blankets around him he finished the last of the Cheezies and stretched out on the floor.

His hunger had become agonizing, and tantalizing pictures of food floated across his mind.

Terrified he would drift off in the freezing hell, he struggled to stay awake by moving his body and counting the hours aloud. The day and night passed slowly.

To keep fear at bay, he tried to remember some of his childhood prayers, long since abandoned. 'Now I lay me down to sleep' ran through his mind. But he was too exhausted to concentrate. Eventually he was unable to fight off sleep any longer, and sank into a state of semi-consciousness.

It was a restless sleep. He could hear the muffled chanting of the cadavers under the snow, enticing him to join them in their icy graves. They called out their names in terrifying monotones. Then the dream changed into ravenous packs of wolves circling the plane.

Awake, he threw off his blanket and jumped out into the frozen night. He ran to the edge of the lake and onto the ice, fleeing his gruesome tormentors. When he could run no longer, he grew calmer. He trudged wearily back to the plane, settled down and tried to sleep.

Awake or asleep, he could not keep the singing cadavers or howling wolves from invading his confused mind.

After a long night, he awoke to day four. Exhausted and ravenously hungry, he huddled beneath the blankets inside the plane, awaiting his fate. Suddenly he was wide awake and hyperalert. He heard a muffled whirring. He lay still for a moment, uncertain. Maybe he was just hallucinating again. But the whirring sounds grew closer and louder.

He recognized the spin of propeller blades as the chopper descended. His heart raced with excitement. He crawled out of the tangle of blankets on hands and knees, and with a mighty effort, threw himself out into the snow. He lay under the Otter's wings, catching his breath and flailing his limp arms, as the long, white fangs of melting icicles drip-dripped down on him. Frantically, he strained to shout "I'm here! I'm here!" But his words came in hoarse whispers.

He watched the Griffon drop low.

It landed on the nearby frozen lake.

Relief washed over him like a suffocating wave. Unable to feel his feet, and barely able to stand, he willed his rubbery legs to plow through the snow towards the helicopter, but soon collapsed in defeat. Frantically, he forced himself along on his stomach, pushing forward inch by inch. Every few minutes he would disappear, as if he'd fallen into a hole, only to reappear again fighting through the deep drifts. Cold and miserable, his body wasn't in it. He just wanted to lie down and sleep, but the thought of rescue, so agonizingly close, galvanized him and he clawed his way forward toward salvation.

Rescue pilot Bill Harvey had seen the crude SOS laid out in the snow, and the outline of the Otter. Setting down, he saw the three snowy mounds scattered near the plane and he surmised what lay beneath.

But he knew there were five people on the plane. Could anyone still be alive in that mess?

Suddenly, he focused on the snow. Someone, or something, was definitely on the move, heading slowly toward him. As Joe inched closer, Bill could scarcely believe his eyes. He leaped out of the chopper, and bounded through the deep snowdrifts toward Joe's half-frozen body. He lifted him up, and carried him back into the warmth of the Griffon's cockpit. He sat down with Joe in his arms, willing warmth into his frozen limbs. He wrapped him in a blanket, and settled him into the co-pilot's seat.

Enlivened by the warmth inside the cockpit, Joe turned his numb face to Bill.

"What... took you?" he croaked in a show of bravado he didn't feel. "Freezin'... out here..." His teeth chattered. His hunger was ravenous.

Bill handed him a box of sandwiches and a thermos of coffee. "Heck of a place to go ice fishing, Joe," he said softly, looking around the bleak landscape.

Joe smiled with barred teeth. "Yeah," he mumbled, biting shakily into a sandwich. "Didn't have much choice." He cradled a cup of hot coffee in his stiff fingers, relishing the warmth. He was sheepishly aware that his clothing reeked, and he was in desperate need of a long hot shower. Bill watched him carefully.

"You're alone, I guess?"

Joe nodded slowly chewing his sandwich in silence.

"And those are what I think they are?" he asked, pointing to three snow mounds near the stricken Otter. He tried to sound hopeful, but didn't feel it.

"Yeah," Joe said.

"Well, I've got to get them now, Joe. Another storm like this one and they'll be buried till spring."

Joe nodded, gulping coffee and slowly warming up. Haltingly, he recounted his ordeal.

Bill listened in amazement.

"You're one lucky bastard," he muttered, patting him on the back. "Stay here and thaw out. I'll manage the bodies."

Bill brushed snow from the four rigid bodies and wrapped them in the blankets Joe had used during the long frigid nights. He loaded the bodies of Pete and Tim into the side baskets of the helicopter, strapping them in. He placed the Inuit woman and her baby inside the helicopter, their bodies frozen together. Back inside, Bill prepared for take-off and radioed the hospital they were on their way.

"Okay, we're off," he called out. But Joe had already fallen asleep, basking in soothing warmth and a full stomach.

In a few hours, they landed their ill-fated cargo in Edmonton. A waiting ambulance whisked Joe to the hospital. The bodies were taken to the morgue.

It remained a mystery how Joe had survived the crash. In the days to come, he often wondered if he really did freeze to death, but by some miracle had returned to life to be rescued.

Was there a lesson to be learned from it all, or was it just a random twist of fate? If an answer existed, Joe never dared look for it, on the theory that sometimes it's enough just to be alive.

A Summer of Sorrow

Decaying, reeking bodies
Stacked like cordwood
On the hard, rocky ground
Cries of "water, water"
Rustled the sour air
Like a zephyr wind

Out in the Gulf
Miles of coffin ships
Plugged the bay
Bearing a sickly cargo
A diaspora of fleeing Irish
Fugitives from poverty and pestilence

Hope beckoned in a new world
But misery was their welcome
Disease became their stalker
Fate snatched away their dreams

Helen McCourt Mentek

The raging tide could not be stemmed
By medicine or prayer
Many thousands clutched at life
But death won the uneven race

The strong survived
To kiss the cold lips of loved ones
Buried them in rough coffins
Three-tiered deep

They dug the graves
With sorrowing hearts
And wept their silent tears

The Wild Geese

The village of Skibbereen resembled many other villages in the County of West Cork, and it was much the same throughout Ireland during the terrible years of the famine. The population of the ill-fated country endured numbing poverty, excluding no one. Even the animals, or what was left of them, were bone-thin.

The endless misery continued to hold the nation in its grip. For generations, the potato had been the staple of the Irish diet, but now it had become a slimy decaying mess unfit to eat. Crops had been decimated by a blight that had crossed into Ireland from southern England. The earth was covered with rotting stinking vegetation as far as the eye could see. Men, women and children were thrown into destitution and starvation with no relief in sight. No one in the land was spared.

The tiny cottages dotting the desolate landscape mirrored each other. The peeling whitewashed walls and the thatches on the roofs were all in desperate need of a caring hand. Inside the cottages, the only ventilation, apart from the door, was a hole in the straw roof to allow the smoke to escape from the turf fire inside. The interior was always dim and smoky. Very few could afford the luxury of windows because a hefty tax was imposed, adding to the rent. Local agents hired by absentee landlords collected the rents from the tenants, and very often with force. If there was no money for payment, and often there was not, the residents were immediately evicted. Everywhere were clusters of roofless, empty cabins. Former inhabitants were dead and buried in pauper's graves, or, if they were lucky, had escaped across the Atlantic to the New World. Many who were unable to leave Ireland were reduced to living under a tree or in a cave dug out of the earth.

The survival of many hung by a thread.

So it was in the Boland cottage. Despite the fire blazing in the grate, the morning's sudden chill had plunged the family cottage into an aura of deep melancholy. The aged couple huddled close to the hearth, their gnarled hands reaching out toward the flames in a vain attempt to coax a little warmth into their emaciated bodies.

Young Patrick Boland stood on the hard-packed dirt floor of the cottage. His solid physique overwhelmed the room. He stood out in stark contrast to his parents, now shrunken and old beyond their years. His black curls bounced as he slowly shook his head and gazed at them with a mixture of love and sadness. Anguish was etched on Patrick's face. His lips trembled as he beheld their gaunt faces, weather-beaten and grooved. He knew his time had come to leave, but he was torn between wanting to go and dreading it. Something inside him said "Don't do it", and yet he knew there was no alternative. He had to go to save them both from starvation. He would be another "bread and butter" immigrant.

"So, it's come then," his mother said in a quivering voice as she rose slowly from her stool. They had talked and argued about this day for months and now it was here. Patrick was always adamant to stay but his parents insisted he must go. The boy was only seventeen years old and had very little formal schooling. All the regular schools in the country had been closed by an English proclamation, and the head-masters thrown out or jailed if they tried to defy the law. Under great secrecy, schools were organized behind the hedgerows by a few coura-geous teachers who were known as "hedge-masters." These men and women were dedicated teachers who refused to stand by and watch a generation of Irish youth become illiterate.

The oppressive law denied anyone the opportunity to learn to read or write. Ironically, before the English suppression, the Irish clergy had been writing and reading books for centuries. Irish monks of long ago had been translating biblical texts and history into the Celtic language. They were known as the "saviours of civilization," while, at the same time, British savages were running through the forests covering themselves in blue paint. But the philistines had become the oppressors, and as a symbol of their authority, had contrived a means to systematically purge the Irish people by starvation and ignorance. The result of these laws was a staggering Irish diaspora to the New World.

Much of the Irish youth left the homeland and their families and crossed the Atlantic to North America. From there they could work and send money to assist those they left behind, now too old or sick to leave.

Patrick's father, Daniel, struggled to his feet and extended his hand to his son. He saw the uncertainty in Patrick's face.

"It'll be all right, lad. God will walk with you," his father said in a comforting tone.

"But da, how will you manage alone?"

"Well now, Canada is not another world, is it, son?" He tried to cover his pain with a smile. In his heart, he didn't want his only child to leave. He was fearful of the kind of life that lay before the young man. It seemed like only yesterday Patrick was a happy "spalpeen," playing in the yard with old Pete, his dog, or helping his pa with the hoeing. How would he get on? Would he be safe? But Daniel kept his silence.

"When you've settled yerself somewhere, boy, let us know where you be. God willing, we'll still be here." His father nodded his head with certainty.

Maeve, his mother, fought back her tears. Her wrinkled face was pinched, defying one teardrop to fall onto her cheek. She would not see her son leave his home anxious with worry about them. She was keenly aware she might never see him again but pushed that thought out of her mind. She kissed him on the cheek and blessed him with a splash of holy water from a small bottle. From her apron, she pulled out a wee cloth bag.

"Keep this safe about yer person, love" she murmured, pressing it into his hand.

Patrick fingered the coins inside the bag.

"No, ma. I'll not take this," he said, his eyes fixed on his mother firmly. "Sure you'll be needin' it for yerselves." He tried to press it back into her hands but she turned away and would not take it.

"We'll manage, son." His father spoke softly, grabbing Patrick's hand in his bony fingers. "You can't be goin' about the world with yer mind troubled, and no jingle in yer pockets." He withdrew his hand and hugged his son with all the strength of his frail arms. Patrick turned to his mother, his eyes full of tears. She held him close, not wanting to let him go. Reluctantly, he pulled himself away from her thin body. He closed his eyes, unable to look at her, his pain was so intense.

The little cottage was the only home he had ever known. He crossed the threshold not daring to look back. Choking back sobs, he raised his hand in a final farewell. Soon his backpack was out of sight. He strode on boldly, his father's walking stick secure in his hand, his passage papers hidden in his cap.

The Boland's landlord had paid for Patrick's passage to Canada. Oddly, there were some compassionate landlords who would pay for the passage of any man or boy who wanted to emigrate. It was widely believed that if some of the young and healthy were to leave, it would stem the rising tide of death that was raging across the country and rid Ireland of some of its misery.

After several days of walking and sleeping in any shelter he could find, Patrick arrived in the town of Cork. He took his passage papers to the ship assigned to him and boarded with several hundred other passengers awaiting the crossing to North America.

Hope for a better life was the theme of conversations among the passengers. But as it happened, many of them fell sick before they left Ireland. Over the course of the three-month journey there were countless shipboard deaths. Their bodies were dumped into the sea without any spiritual ceremony unless there happened to be a priest on hand.

Patrick was immediately aware of the overwhelming sickness in the hold of the ship when he descended with the other passengers.

Gaunt bodies were packed in the airless stinking confine. People were sleeping inches from one another. Some looked as though they would never rise again from the straw mattresses in their bunks. Patrick backed away from sharing a bunk with a possibly sick person and he made a bed of straw on the floor. For much of the voyage he stayed there, conserving his energy and keeping his distance from the others. The passengers were allowed up on deck for fresh air and exercise every day and Patrick took every advantage of that, lingering in the open air until he was chased back down into the hold by the crew.

As the ship sailed on, Patrick passed his seventeenth birthday. He struggled to hold back his tears, as he recalled past celebrations with his parents and legions of aunts, uncles and cousins. He was an only child and he had always relished his special day, impatiently awaiting it. If all went well on his journey to the New World and he didn't succumb to the sickness around him, he would see his future birthdays in a new land.

Food and water were handed out by the captain each day. Everyone received seven pounds of food a week and a little water, but sometimes there wasn't enough to go around. The captain kept much of it for himself and his crew. Much of the water was contaminated and undrinkable because it was kept in old wine or chemical casks. Food was constantly being stolen by the desperate and was the cause of many fights and sometimes even murder.

After three months of sailing, Patrick's ship, the *Virginius,* arrived at the shores of North America. They anchored at Grosse Isle, just off the coast of Quebec. An order was given for all passengers to stay on board, while a medical officer from the Canadian immigration station rowed out to examine them for symptoms of typhus. The sick were detained and the ship was disinfected along with its contents. The very ill and the dying were carried off and transported to a makeshift hospital on the island. The dead were removed later and buried in paupers' graves.

Everyone who was free of the disease and physically able to leave the ship descended rope ladders down the side of the ship. There were no docking facilities at the tiny island.

The survivors dropped down into the shallow water, the young helping the old.

They clambered over the rocks, and headed for a myriad of tents where a few doctors separated the sick from the healthy. The makeshift shelters were crowded with emaciated people looking for food and rest.

Doctors on duty in the hospital tents examined the women and children first. A long queue of bone-weary men stood silently, awaiting their turn.

Finally, Patrick reached the head of the line. With no typhus evident, he was deemed fit to leave the island.

He picked up his meagre bundle of possessions and a small packet of food that everyone was given upon leaving the island, and he strode into the unknown.

He had walked about a mile when he encountered two young men reclining on a bank of grass beside the road, eating from a brown paper bag. Patrick stopped to ask directions. He was told they had recently arrived on a ship from Sligo, Ireland.

"Would yez be kind enough to tell me how to get shut of this terrible place?" Patrick asked.

They told him they were looking for a barge to transport them up the St. Lawrence River to Montreal.

"Would you be wantin' to join us lad?" one of them spoke up. "Pleased we would be for your company." He stuck out his hand. "Me name is Michael Walsh and this here fella is James O'Connor." He pointed to his companion and they all shook hands.

"I'm Patrick Boland from Skibbereen and I'm very pleased to know ya. I'm not sure at all just where I'm headed, but I would be glad to join ya. Do you know where we are now?"

"No, lad. Nor have we ever set foot in this God-forsaken place before today, and the sooner we get away from it the better. Sure and Montreal can't be more than a good spit from here."

He stood up and motioned toward the road. "Walk along with us. This is the road we were told that leads to the docks where the barges are berthed."

They walked along in companionable chatter, exchanging stories about their lives in Ireland and how the famine had forced them to leave. The breezes were refreshing after the close confines on ship and they filled their lungs with the fresh air. After a couple of hours of walking, they came to a small fishing village. In the harbour they could see long lines of barges. Some were docked, and some were pulling away loaded with people.

"Thanks be to God, this be the place," Michael exclaimed. "Let's get onto one of them contraptions and get shut of this place. Sure a ride is always better than walking, is it not?" he added, laughing.

"Should we not try to get some food to take along with us?" Patrick suggested.

"Good thinking," replied Michael. "Let's try in the village to buy or beg. Begging is better," he added with a grin.

They each chose a different house, knocked on several doors, asking to buy some food from the residents. The homeowners looked at their ragged and thin figures, and after a few spoken words became aware of their origin. The residents would not take their money and loaded them up with potatoes, tea, apples, bread and from some of the more generous, packages of dried fish.

"We are quite willing to pay," Patrick insisted.

"There is never a charge for hospitality to our brothers," they replied in heavy Irish accents.

Amid cries of "Thanks. Good-bye" and "Good luck" the trio reached the docks. For a few pennies they boarded one of the barges and shortly after, were on their way up the St. Lawrence.

Montreal Harbour was bustling with men unloading goods. People were disembarking from all manners of transportation. Patrick was curious about all the hustle-bustle around him and a bit overwhelmed by the noise and shouting among the workers. The three boys decided to split up to search for work and shelter for the oncoming night. Patrick walked around the town. He came across a sign tacked to the front of a building advertising "Rooms for Rent." He walked through the open door and approached a woman sitting at table in the hall.

"I would like to rent a room for tonight if you please, missus," he said.

Instantly, she recognized his broad accent and answered, "That'll be 25 cents for the night".

Extending her hand, she added, "I'm Mrs. Mulligan. What part of Ireland are you from, lad?"

As they talked, they discovered they had lived a few miles from each other in County Cork. She took an immediate liking to Patrick and told him she had been in Montreal for ten years, as she gave him a motherly inspection.

"You must be done in from all your travels," she added. "Get yerself a bath and some sleep, and we'll talk about what to do with you a little later over some supper." She handed him a key and said, "Take room number two. The number's on the door. The bath is down the hall." As Patrick stood up, she added, "You'll be needin' some decent clothes if you're wantin' a job. Nobody'll hire you lookin' like the divil hisself," she added.

"I have a bit put by, ma'am. Tomorrow, I'll get me a few things," he told her.

While he slept, Mrs. Mulligan gathered up all his dirty clothes and washed them. She hung them on the clothesline at the back of her house. When he awoke, she gave him an old bathrobe to cover himself, while she fixed him some supper.

They sat together at her kitchen table. She poured the tea and set out some bread and cheese for him. He was ravenous but tried not to bolt it down and embarrass himself.

"While I was at the grocer's earlier, I asked what employment might be available nearby," she told him. "Mr. Kowalski told me he'd heard they were hiring over in Lachine for work on the new canal. They're digging the canal deeper so the bigger ships can come through. Also, he said if you went right away you would likely get work that would last for perhaps a year or so. Would that be of interest to you, Patrick?"

"It would, indeed," Patrick exclaimed. He was eager to work anywhere so he could begin a new life in this country, and send money back to his parents.

One of Mrs. Mulligan's boarders was working in Lachine and she arranged for Patrick to ride out with him in the morning.

"God bless you, ma'am. Sure and it's a saint you are."

"Ah, get on with you, lad. I hope you have good luck." They talked until Patrick started to nod off again. She gathered his dried clothes from the line and handed them to him. "Get back to bed, son. You'll be needin' all the rest you can get for tomorrow."

The following morning Patrick stood before the canal boss. He was worried he was not making a good impression. He knew he needed a haircut and new clothes but there had been no time. Fortunately, the man only saw Patrick's brawny frame, and with a nod said, "You'll do fine," and extended his hand. As they shook hands on the deal, Patrick was unable to control his smile.

"See the supervisor over there." The boss pointed to a man standing by an empty truck. "He'll tell you what your duties will be." Patrick approached the supervisor. "I've just been hired on," he told him. "What will I be doing?"

"Grab a shovel and start loading that pile of sludge into this here truck," he growled. "We'll all take a break in a few hours. You can get yourself a cup of tea from the wagon over yonder." He walked off checking his clipboard with a pencil he took from behind his ear.

For several years Patrick labored at the canal site, earning money to send his parents in Ireland. He stayed with the job, working hard and eventually rising to supervisor. This meant more money and responsibility which he handled with steady confidence.

He scrupulously saved every penny he could, and continued to send money home. It was all that kept his mother and father alive during the ongoing years of deprivation. He was determined to settle in and make this country his home. His goal was to start up his own construction business.

One evening, he attended a dance at the local church hall with a couple of men from the boarding house. He stood on the fringe of the dancers wanting to join in, but feeling a little shy about asking anyone to dance.

As he watched the whirling bodies, his eyes were drawn to a lively girl on the dancefloor. It was her long black hair that caught his eye as she circled the floor with her partner, her hair fanning out from the momentum. When the dance ended, she rejoined her friends. Patrick couldn't take his eyes off her and finally found the courage to approach.

"Would you care to dance with me, miss," he asked tentatively.

She looked him over, recognized the word "dance" and replied in French. "Ah, oui. Je voudrais bien." She smiled and held out her hands.

Patrick figured her answer must have meant yes.

They stepped into the fray and joined in a folk dance. Patrick was a bit unsure, but as the dance progressed it seemed very much like an Irish reel and he soon picked up the tempo. As they danced they introduced themselves. She said her name was Adèle Fontaine.

When the last dance ended and the hall emptied, they stepped out into the night together.

"May I walk you home, Adèle?"

Adèle could understand a little English she had learned from her father who worked in an English machine shop in Lachine, but she was not able to give Patrick an answer in English.

"Oui, oui! J'amerais bien ca!" she exclaimed, nodding her head vigorously. She took his arm and they headed off to her home a couple of blocks away.

As they walked, they tried to communicate with each other, mostly in sign language. There was much laughing and pointing in their conversation. When they arrived at Adèle's home, she turned to Patrick and said, "No inviter," shaking her head. "I must en parler à papa. Mais, come Sunday après la messe," she added.

Patrick understood her invitation for Sunday.

"I'll be there with bells on," he said, grinning.

She stared at him, utterly perplexed.

"Alright, I won't wear bells!" he laughed.

They parted, and Adèle waved to him from the veranda.

The following Sunday, Patrick knocked on her door. He wore a new suit with a sparkling white shirt and bow tie. He surely was a princely sight.

Adèle answered the door and ushered him into the parlour. "Venez, venez," she said taking his arm.

Her parents stood side by side looking him over discreetly. Adèle made the introductions, and her father extended his hand.

"Entrez, entrez. Sit, s'il vous plaît," he said in a loud voice. Madame Fontaine indicated a chair to a very nervous Patrick.

The atmosphere was a little strained at first, each trying to communicate in two different languages. Monsieur Fontaine spoke first in halting English.

"Adèle say you work on canal, non?"

"Yes I do, sir." Patrick replied.

"What work 'ave you?"

"Well," Patrick replied with a big grin, "I was just made supervisor."

"Tres bien! Je vous félicite!" Monsieur Fontaine was evidently impressed with Patrick and his work ethic.

The conversation was centered on their work at the canal, where both were employed. Each had a limited knowledge of the other's language and they were only able to discuss their work, and the politics of the company, in a somewhat restricted fashion. Patrick told him of his plans to start his own construction business in the future. Monsieur Fontaine raised his eyebrows in surprise.

"Vous êtes ambitieux, c'est certain," he said smiling.

Adèle and her mother returned from the kitchen with a tray of coffee and cakes.

She offered the tray to Patrick, and said, "Servez-vous, monsieur."

She pointed to the cream and sugar on the tray. Patrick settled back with a mug of coffee and a hefty slice of fruit cake. "Merci, madame," he murmured.

He wanted to make a good impression on her family, and so there were many such Sundays at the Fontaine home after mass and many more dances and walks for Patrick and Adèle.

Over many months they fell in love and made plans to marry. But first, as was the custom, Patrick had to obtain her father's permission.

One evening after a walk, Adèle and Patrick returned to her house to seek her father's approval. When the preliminary greetings with her family were over, Patrick posed the question.

"Monsieur Fontaine," he announced in a firm voice. "Adèle and I love each other very much, and I would like your permission to marry her."

Monsieur Fontaine pursed his lips, and mulled over the question in his mind. After all, he thought, Patrick isn't French, and we don't really know about his family back in Ireland. He seems like a decent enough fellow, though, and Adèle is clearly in love with him. He also knew that his daughter had the will-power to marry even if he did not give his permission. Also, Patrick was a Catholic and a regular church-goer. He pondered as these thoughts and others ran through his mind.

Meanwhile, Patrick sat in increasing trepidation. Finally, Monsieur Fontaine spoke.

"Bien. Je vous donne ma bénédiction," he said, smiling. "Prenez soin d'elle, Patrick. Never 'urt her, vous comprenez? Jamais!! I 'ope you are 'appy, both. Que Dieu vous bénisse."

"Thank you, sir. I would never hurt Adèle, ever! I love her too much. Never fear, I will take good care of her all her life with me." He stood up and held out his hand.

The deal was sealed.

There was much to do to prepare for the wedding. Finally, the big day arrived and Patrick and Adèle became husband and wife in the church they both attended.

They settled into their new home. Monsieur Fontaine had helped to purchase a very nice little cottage for their first adventure in married life.

Soon there were children, three in quick succession.

Patrick was blessed and he knew it. But always, he longed to return to Ireland to see his parents, who had survived thanks to the money he'd sent over the years. He had written them that he had married, and sent tintype portraits of Adèle and the children. Still, he was haunted by the feeling that he must return soon, or it might be too late to see them alive.

By now he had established himself in his construction business, and was financially able to take the trip with the children and Adèle. It was just a question of whether she would want to go. The farthest she had been from Lachine was to Montreal with her parents.

He broached the subject one evening after the children were in bed.

"Adèle dear, I'm thinking of going to Ireland soon, with you and the children, so they can meet their other grandparents. What do you think of that idea?"

She stared at him not knowing what to say. In the back of her mind, she knew that someday he may want to go back, but even so, his idea came like a bolt from the blue.

After a moment's pause, she said, "That's a wonderful idea, Patrick. They should know their other grandparents as well as mama and papa Fontaine, and I also would like to meet them. When could we go?"

"I'll arrange passports for all of us, and for a ship to take us to Cork. I'll get some transportation for us, too, and we will be in Skibbereen before you know it," he replied, smiling at the thought.

Over the next few weeks the house was a great flurry of activity as they prepared for the trip. The children were in a constant state of excitement at the thought of sailing on a big ship across the ocean, and pestered their father with questions. They were all of school age now, and could follow exactly where they were going on their school maps.

Finally, all the paperwork arrived and Patrick proceeded to book a ship.

In the middle of dinner one evening, there was a knock at the door. A young messenger boy stood outside.

"You Patrick Boland?" he asked.

"I am," Patrick replied.

"I have a message for you from Ireland." He held out an envelope.

"How did you get a message for me from Ireland?" Patrick asked.

"From the ship," was the answer.

Patrick looked dumbfounded and the lad went on to explain.

"Messages come on the food ships when they come back here."

"Well, I thank you, son," Patrick nodded to the lad. He handed him a few coins for his trouble.

He closed the door and tore open the envelope. As he read the words, he cried out. Adèle rushed to his side.

"What is it?" she asked. He handed her the letter.

"It's from my cousin. My parents...they've died." He choked back sobs as the tears streamed down his cheeks.

"Oh, mon cher, I'm so sorry." She put her arms around him.

The children, still seated at the table, stared wide-eyed and curious.

"What's wrong, mama. Why is daddy crying?"

"Hush children. Daddy has had some sad news. His parents have gone to heaven."

Patrick read that his parents had passed away within two weeks of each other, and the funeral had already taken place. His cousin had agreed that it was senseless to hold up the burial, as it would be impossible for Patrick to get there in time.

Patrick looked at the date on the letter. Two months had passed since their deaths, and he was only now receiving word of it.

He sat with his head in his hands, his shoulders shaking with grief. Adèle held him in her arms. "They're gone," he said shakily. "My parents are both gone! I should have returned sooner. I could have. Why didn't I?" he groaned.

"You did everything you could for them, Patrick. You were always a good son. You must not blame yourself."

In the days that followed, Patrick kept his passport and a reservation for one, and he set sail alone for his homeland. Three weeks later he arrived in Cork, and caught a ride on a farmer's cart to Skibbereen. He was met there by his cousin, with whom he stayed. People from Skibbereen came to see him to express their condolences.

He made arrangements for a beautifully inscribed marble Celtic cross to be placed at the graves, and then he knelt and prayed for his parents' souls, begging forgiveness for returning too late.

A celebration of Daniel and Maeve Boland's lives was held at his cousin's home. Many nearby relatives and friends came to share his grief. It was there that he learned his parents had helped many others with the money he had sent over the years.

Several years later he brought Adèle and their three children to Ireland and to the little village of Skibbereen. They visited the grave-yard, knelt at his parents' graves and prayed. He returned to Canada with his family, saddened that his children would never know their Irish grandparents.

Back home in Lachine, Patrick's construction business was booming. In a few years, Shamrock Construction Company expanded into Montreal and surrounding areas. His dream was to build homes for the many immigrants arriving in the New World from all over Europe, and later, for Canadian soldiers returning from the First World War.

Patrick Boland's company was one of many success stories of Ireland's "Wild Geese", immigrants who fled the famine to build new lives and futures on Canadian soil.

The Train

We didn't hear the one-eyed monster
Barreling down the tracks
Belching smoke
Flashing fire
Too late to flee
Clickety-clack
Clickety-clack
Clickety-clack
Clickety-clack
Clickety-clack

Winning the Race

It was the summer of 1936, in the middle of the Great Depression, and the Pinchuk's Saskatchewan farm was in trouble. A drought had taken its toll, followed by an infestation of grasshoppers that devastated the wheat fields, leaving the family in poverty. Millions of insects floated in the air until a breeze swept them to the ground, where they devoured everything in sight that was green. Then they moved on to the next farm, and the next, swarming over the fields. The crackling sounds of their destruction could be heard everywhere, turning the once-flourishing prairies into a dustbowl. Many families left their farms and moved to nearby cities to look for work.

Walter Pinchuk couldn't understand why the prairies had betrayed him. They were so good to him at first, and to his father before him. He stood on his verandah looking out at his parched fields, recalling the time he'd arrived in Canada from the Ukraine in the late 1800s with his parents and his brother, Alec, all gone now. Walter was ten, Alec was twelve. He recalled the sod hut they'd helped their father build to shelter them. The following year, they erected a small frame house and the family moved in before the first cold snap of winter. A second storey for bedrooms was added in later years. The sod hut became a temporary home for the family's farm animals until a barn was erected a year later with the help of their neighbours. He remembered how excited he and Alec were when everyone gathered for the barn raising. It was the day he'd first seen the pretty blond eight-year-old Erika Olsen. Years later, after a short courtship, they were married. They lived in the same house he'd helped his father build, and raised two sons, Roy and James.

Roy, the eldest, was twenty years old. His hair was blond and straight, parted in the middle. His skin was so fair that his constant chin stubble was barely visible. He was average height with a slim build that belied his strength. Erika Pinchuk's family had emigrated from Norway and Roy took after her side of the family. He looked nothing like his sibling and was teased mercilessly. James told Roy that their mother had found him under a cabbage leaf in the garden. Playful scuffles resulted until Walter stepped in with jobs he knew they hated, like cleaning the chicken coop and shoveling out the barn.

James was a duplicate of his father. He had Walter's curly black hair, dark eyes, and solid physique. At eighteen, he was a handsome young man. Coal black curls framed a face of perpetual mirth. He had a distinctive loping gait, shoulders swinging from side to side in concert with his stride, the picture of youthful confidence. James was a risk-taker. No job or adventure was too challenging for him, and his many harrowing escapades on the farm exasperated his parents. But James laughed it all off.

Walter Pinchuk was fifty-three years old, and very proud of his sons. He was a tall, thin, raw-boned man. Graying wavy hair framed the leathery skin of his face, lined with deep wrinkles. As he stared out at wheat fields crumbling into dust before his eyes, a great sadness hung over him like a shroud. He realized he had nothing left to give them. Tears ran down his cheeks. He closed his eyes and raised a clenched fist to the sky.

"How will we ever survive?" he cried out.

He felt he had failed them all.

Erika tried to reassure him. She stood by him, a tall, slim woman of fifty years. Her once blond hair, now faded to silver, was braided in a coronet on top of her head. Her fair complexion was freckled from many hot prairie summers but still held some of the freshness of her youth.

"You can't stop hoping, Walt," she'd say. "We'll see it through… together." But every day, he became more and more despondent as the drought continued and the farm plunged deeper into debt.

When Roy and James approached their father with a plan to leave the farm and look for work elsewhere, Walter was at first angry and refused to discuss it. Erika, too, thought it best if the boys stayed home, and waited for better times. She thought there were too many men out searching for work, and some of them were not to be trusted. She feared for their safety, and remained hopeful that they would find odd jobs in the nearby town of Evansville. But there never were any. The situation became so desperate that Walt was forced to accept their sons' plan. He hoped they could find work somewhere, and help pull the farm out of debt.

The day they left, their parents cautioned them. "You have to watch out for yourselves. You're going far from home…strange places… strange people. Take care of each other."

And so, early one September morning, Roy and James left the farm, and walked two miles down the dirt road to the Evansville train station. They carried knapsacks with a few extra clothes and a little food and water. They were familiar with the schedules of freight trains passing daily through the town. They had been planning this adventure for weeks.

James found an empty boxcar and they climbed in, settling down in a corner out of sight. Before long they heard hoarse voices shouting as the cars were shunted onto an engine. A trainman, who didn't notice them huddled inside, slid the door and slammed it shut, and the train moved on.

Roy scrambled up to check the door. It was unlocked. He breathed a sigh of relief. The train picked up speed and they were off. They pressed together for comfort and warmth. They ate a little food, and soon the swaying and click-clacking of the wheels on the rails lulled them to sleep.

In the morning, they were awakened by the jolting and creaking of the engine's brakes, bringing the train to a stop. Roy crept to the door and opened it a crack. He looked around. The station sign said 'Coopers' Landing'.

"I'll wait here with our stuff," he said to James. "You go and get us some food."

James walked along the main street of Coopers' Landing, in Ontario, knocking on doors. He asked for food and water, with little success. He almost gave up hope of getting anything. But at the last house, a young girl opened the door. For a moment, he was tongue-tied. The farm girls back home were thin and work-worn, but this girl was tall and blonde with pretty blue eyes. Her crisp blue shirt was tucked into a white skirt—and her sporty white oxfords looked brand new. James felt hugely embarrassed by his wrinkled and soiled farm overalls. And he knew his personal hygiene was far from present-able. He ran his fingers through his black curls, hoping to improve his disheveled appearance.

In a low voice, he stammered, "Please miss, could you give us something to eat and some water?"

Her blue eyes twinkled. "What do you mean, 'us'? I only see one of you." Her voice was soft and teasing.

"I mean, me and my brother," James muttered. "We've been riding the rails all night and ..." hunger gave his voice some courage, "...we're really hungry, miss."

"Sure," she said, and motioned him to the veranda steps. "Wait there, and I'll make some sandwiches. Enough for both of you... if there really are two of you," she added, grinning.

"It's not a lie," he exclaimed. "My brother's waiting back at the station. He's watching our stuff."

"Okay, I'll be right back," she said, and she vanished behind the closing door.

In a few minutes, the door opened, and she held out a paper bag of sandwiches and apples.

"I put some tea in there, too. Maybe you can get some hot water somewhere."

"Thanks miss," James said, reaching for the bag. He turned and walked down the sidewalk, looking back wistfully.

The train was pulling out. James began to run alongside the slowly moving car. He threw himself inside, gasping for breath.

Roy opened the bag and they ate the sandwiches. The train puffed on, loaded with enough coal and water to travel through the night. They drifted off to sleep.

In the morning, they awoke to the train's creaking noises as it slowed to a stop. Roy peered through a crack in the door. The station sign said **Beauchene**.

"Come on James," he shouted. We're pulling into a station." James sat up rubbing his eyes. He ran his hands through his tangled hair and yawned a question. "Where the hell are we, Roy?"

Roy looked closer at the sign. "I don't know. But I know we ain't nowhere near Coopers' Landing. I think we're in Quebec. We have to go back." Unable to speak French, they believed it was useless to look for work here. They waited at the station, until they saw a train heading back to Ontario. It stopped at the coal chute long enough for them to find an empty car and climb in. They huddled together in a corner out of sight. Soon the familiar shunting and screeching sounds told them they were leaving.

The train rattled on for a short time. The first stop was a town called Hoskins' Corners. James jumped off to ask for food and water. Roy stayed behind to watch their belongings. Theft was a way of life in these hard times, and all they owned was in those two knapsacks. It was late when James arrived back at the station, with a can of water and a bag of sandwiches. The train jolted and shuddered as it moved forward. James started to run alongside as the train picked up speed. He fell behind.

"C'mon James," Roy shouted from inside the box car. James sprinted forward, his eyes on Roy's outstretched hand.

He couldn't reach it.

He stumbled. His legs slid under the wheels. The engineer suddenly brought the train to a screeching halt. James lay on the tracks, his legs mangled and bloody. Roy jumped down and raced down the tracks, screaming, "James... James, hang on, I'm comin'."

He stared frozen in horror at James's mutilated body, his outstretched hand still clutching a bag of sandwiches. For a moment, nothing moved but the tears streaming down Roy's face. He began to tremble violently. Choking sobs rumbled from his throat. He slid in beside James and cradled his head in his arms.

"C'mon, brother. Don't die on me," he bawled. "Breathe, dammit, breathe. Please James, breathe."

The stationmaster, seeing the disruption on the tracks, called the police. A squad car arrived immediately. An ambulance followed, sirens screaming.

John Holmes, an elderly gentleman standing on the station platform, saw it all. He hurried to the scene. Roy was sitting on the ground in shock. John stood beside him while James was lifted into the ambulance. A policeman slammed the door and rapped a 'ready signal'. The driver sped away, sirens open.

Roy sat in the Holmes' living room with John and his wife, Jenny. He held a small glass of brandy.

His hands were shaking so badly he couldn't raise it to his lips.

"What's your name, son?" John asked softly.

Roy took a deep shuddering breath. "Roy ... Roy Pinchuk."

"Did you know the boy in the accident?"

Roy nodded. He swallowed hard. "He's my brother, James," he whispered, his eyes lowered.

"Oh! How awful," Jenny exclaimed.

"Where are you from, Roy?" John asked.

"Saskatchewan ... we were ... we were looking for work."

He sat motionless, staring at the knapsacks at his feet, and trying to hang onto everything that kept floating around him.

"Oh, you poor boy," Jenny murmured, taking his hand. "We'll take you to the hospital when you're ready."

John called the Hoskins' Corners hospital for information, but James carried no identification, and no one knew who he was, or where he had come from.

They sat in the waiting room anxious for news until a doctor saw them sitting together. He approached them. "Mr. Holmes?" he asked. "Is the boy in the accident your son?"

"No," John replied. "He is this boy's brother. They were on the train together. His name is Roy Pinchuk. His brother is James Pinchuk. They came together from their farm near Evansville, Saskatchewan."

The doctor turned to Roy. He put a hand on his shoulder. "I'm sorry to have to tell you, Roy, that your brother didn't survive the accident. We did everything we could to save him but there was too much damage and blood loss."

"He's dead?" Roy whispered hoarsely. "James is dead?

Doctor Grayson looked at the frightened boy. "I'm so sorry," he said.

"Oh, no, please, God. Please," Roy moaned. He held his head in his hands, sobbing.

Dr. Grayson motioned to John.

"Can you identify the body?" he asked.

John shook his head. "I've never met the lad and Roy can't do it right now, Doctor. I'll take him home with me to rest, and come with him tomorrow."

Roy had passed out. Jenny was struggling to hold him on the seat.

"John," she called. "Help me."

They placed Roy's limp body on a sofa. In a few minutes, he began to come around and tried to sit up.

"No, Roy, stay there," the doctor said, beckoning to a nurse.

"Get him some water," he said, "and stay with him until he is able to leave." He turned to John. "I have to go, but I'll call at your home this evening. Give the nurse your address."

Roy tried to stand, but a wave of dizziness swept over him and he was forced to sit down again.

"I'll get a wheelchair and call a cab for you," the nurse said. "Give him two of these when you get home. He'll sleep for a few hours."

John wheeled Roy outside to a waiting taxi.

At home, he settled Roy in bed in the spare room. Jenny held a glass of water to his lips and he swallowed the tablets. She spread a blanket over him. He was so exhausted that sleep came quickly.

They left the bedroom and went downstairs to make plans to get in touch with Roy's family.

"We'll contact the police here," John said. "They can get in touch with the Evansville police."

Jenny was deep in thought. "Their parents could come here to be with Roy, and they could all go home together with James's body."

"They could, yes. But they may not be in a position to travel. Their farm must be in desperate shape for these boys to have to leave."

At the police station, the duty constable called the Evansville police, who agreed to inform the boy's parents of Roy's whereabouts and James's death.

John asked the local officer for the Pinchuk's address, and handed it to Jenny. "We'll invite the Pinchuks to come here. We'll let them decide on a plan that's best for them."

Back home, John went upstairs to check on Roy, while Jenny took a pen and paper from the desk drawer and wrote a note at the kitchen table.

Dear Mr. & Mrs. Pinchuk.

No doubt by now you have received the tragic news of your son James's accident. My husband and I are deeply sorry for your loss. We want to help you get your family back home.

At present, James's body is at the hospital here in Hoskins' Corners. Roy is here with us. You may stay with us until you can return to Saskatchewan with your sons, or if you prefer, John can escort Roy and James home to you. We want to do everything we can to help you in this sorrowful time.

We will wait to hear what you decide to do.

Enclosed is our telephone number. Please call us collect.

Sincerely,

John and Jenny Holmes

As Jenny was sealing the envelope, Roy sank onto a kitchen chair. He was dressed and ready to go out.

"How are you feeling?" Jenny asked anxiously. "Sit for a minute. I fixed you something to eat."

"No. Thanks, but I have to go," Roy said. "I have to take James home." He was groggy and braced both hands on the table as he spoke.

"Oh, this is bad," he moaned. "I mean, James - it's all my fault. My parents, they'll never forgive me."

"Well now, don't you be worrying about that," Jenny said. She set down a plate of food as a knock sounded behind them.

Dr. Grayson stood on the doorstep. Roy stood up as the doctor entered the kitchen. "How are you feeling? Did you get a little rest?" The doctor pumped up the blood pressure bladder as he spoke.

Roy nodded. "Now I have to tell my parents about James, and take him home."

Jenny Holmes spoke up. "Your parents have been informed of everything, Roy. The police have notified them... and I have also written to them. So, for now, we'll wait here until we hear from them. Don't worry. John will take care of everything."

Roy spoke in a whisper. "Thank-you."

Dr. Grayson picked up his bag. "Well Roy, you seem to be in pretty good shape considering everything. If you need anything, give me a call at my office."

In Saskatchewan, the Evansville police constable drove out to the Pinchuk farm to inform them of James's death. Hearing the news, Erika closed her eyes, and a tortured cry flew from her lips.

Walter caught her swaying body, and carried her to the sofa. He sat beside her, rubbing her hands and speaking quietly to the constable. "Please sit down and tell us what you know."

"Roy is staying in Hoskins' Corners, in Ontario, with a Mr. and Mrs. John Holmes. James's body is being held in the hospital morgue. They're awaiting further instructions."

Walter shook his head in despair. He looked up at the constable, his eyes full of guilt.

"You know, Erika didn't want them to go but I was so worried about the damn farm. I couldn't see the dangers ahead ... so I agreed. The boys thought they could get work somewhere so we could keep the farm afloat."

The constable held out his hand. "I'm so sorry for your loss, Mr. Pinchuk. Call me at the station if you need any help." He let himself out.

Erika moved to sit up.

"Don't get up, Erika," he said, pressing her back. He held her in his arms. For a long while they didn't speak. As the cruel reality of James's death washed over her, she buried her face in her hands. "I can't believe this is happening to us. My poor James," she sobbed. She collapsed against the pillow, fighting the awful pictures of James's accident whirling around in her head.

In a state of disembodied shock, they discussed what to do over the next few days. One morning Walter slipped out to the mailbox. "There may be word from Roy," he said. He lifted the lid and pulled out a letter. Waving it in his hand, he ran back to the house.

"Is it from Roy?" Erika asked.

"No, but it's from the Holmes' in Hoskins' Corners," he answered.

"Read it, Walt. Hurry."

Walter read the letter aloud. "Erika, I have to go to the police station. I want to phone these people, and make some arrangements. Will you be all right?"

"Yes. Go. I'll be alright. I'm just glad Roy is safe, and that he's with James," she said.

At the Evansville station, Walter spoke to the same constable. He handed him the letter.

"We just got this from Ontario. Roy is there with Mr. and Mrs. Holmes and James's body is in the hospital there. I'd like to phone them."

"I'll get them for you." The constable dialed the number in the letter.

John Holmes picked up the ringing phone. He spoke for a moment then called Roy over.

Roy told his father about the plans he was making with John.

"Mr. Holmes says he will go back to Saskatchewan with me and ..." he choked... "with me and James. How is mom? Does she blame me? I couldn't save him, dad. I tried so hard."

"No, no, son, we're not blaming anybody. Mom's alright... just anxious to get both of you home."

"Good. I'll write you the day and time we'll get to Evansville. We'll both be home soon."

"Take care of yourself, son. And thank Mr. and Mrs. Holmes for all their help." Roy hung up and turned to John. "Dad thanks you both for everything. So as soon as we get our tickets, we can get going."

The following morning the train rumbled out of Hoskins' Corners. It pulled into Evansville station two days later.

"I can see them on the platform," Roy said, looking out the window. John smiled, glad to have played a part in reuniting this family.

Walter and Erika clasped Roy in their arms. "Thank the Lord you're safe," Walter said. Erika's tears streamed down her cheeks as she held her surviving son.

Roy's voice was muffled. "I'm sorry I couldn't save him, mom. It's my fault. I tried to grab him ... but ... I couldn't ...." His voice broke.

"No, no, Roy," she whispered, "you mustn't feel like that. Accidents happen... could have happened here too. We have to ... to go on as best we can," she paused, her heart breaking, "without him."

Walter turned to John who was holding out his hand. "How can I ever repay you, John?" he said.

"No need for that, Walter. A lot of people had a hand in this. I was just part of the crowd."

"Well, Erika and I thank you from the bottom of our hearts." He glanced at his wife, clinging to Roy. John led Walter aside.

"We'll want to get James's body off the train without his mother seeing anything," John said. "Take them both home and I'll stay here. When you come back for me, we'll get James's body to the funeral home."

"Thanks John. I don't want Erika to see James like that."

Walter joined Erika and Roy on the platform.

Erika's eyes were full of questions. "What about James?" she asked softly.

"John is looking after him. I want to get you and Roy home first."

He put his arm around her and led them to the truck.

They fell into a quiet sadness, as Walter headed to the farm.

As he drove back to the station alone, Walter couldn't hold back the tears he didn't want to shed in front of Erika. He drove slowly, sobbing uncontrollably.

He pulled into the station yard and sat for a minute, wiping his eyes with his fist. John was standing beside the box holding James's body. Walter went inside and phoned the funeral home. The two men waited outside the station, each handling their sorrow in their own way.

The hearse pulled into the parking lot and they set the box inside. Walter sat with his son's body. He stroked the box with his gnarled hands, bowed his head and prayed for strength to endure the days ahead.

Arriving back at the farm, Walter went at once to Erika. She was unable to form the question in her eyes.

"He's at Morton's Funeral Home," he said. "The funeral will be this Saturday at St. Vladimir's."

They sat in silence with John and Roy, each thinking of what lay ahead and how they would bear it.

In the church, Walter, Erika, John and Roy sat together, holding back their grief. Friends shared memories.

"He was a good boy," Erika said, her voice trembling, "Always had a grin on his face." Her voice faded to a whisper. "He wasn't afraid of anything."

Following the interment, everyone returned to the Pinchuk farm. A meal was prepared by women from the church. Neighbours chatted quietly, and men from nearby farms offered to help Walter and Roy with the neglected chores.

As each day passed, the Pinchuk family gradually settled into the routine of farm life. But the loss of their son and brother was always with them. John Holmes stayed on for a few days, to help wherever he could.

The little farm struggled on for three years, until war broke out in September of 1939. Roy joined the Royal Saskatchewan Regiment in 1941, and soon sailed to England. He spent four years in the army but he always remained focused on the farm. His monthly pay consignment enabled Walter to carry out a few small improvements and hire a farm hand. When the war ended, Roy came home unharmed, determined to lift the farm into a paying enterprise. Under his guidance, the wheat fields began to flourish and the farm rose up from the cold ashes of the Depression.

On an early summer morning, Erika stood on her porch, watching heavy black clouds racing overhead. She lifted her face to the raindrops and felt exhilarated by the wetness on her skin.

She held out her hands, as if to welcome back an old friend. But her thoughts were never far from James. With a heavy heart, she turned and walked briskly back into the house.